Copyright © 2004 by Michael Neugebauer Verlag, an imprint of Nord-Süd Verlag AG, Gossau Zürich, Switzerland
First published in Switzerland under the title Tim Tölpel.
English translation copyright © 2004 by North-South Books Inc., New York
All rights reserved. No part of this book may be reproduced or utilized in any form or by any means,
electronic or mechanical, including photocopying, recording, or any information storage
and retrieval system, without permission in writing from the publisher.
First published in the United States, Great Britain, Canada, Australia, and New Zealand in 2004
by North-South Books, an imprint of Nord-Süd Verlag AG, Gossau Zürich, Switzerland.
Distributed in the United States by North-South Books Inc., New York.
Library of Congress Cataloging-in-Publication Data is available.
A CIP catalogue record for this book is available from The British Library.
ISBN 0-7358-1947-5 (trade edition)
1 2 3 4 5 6 7 8 9 10
ISBN 0-7358-1948-3 (library edition)
1 2 3 4 5 6 7 8 9 10
Printed in Denmark

Author's Note: *Who ever saw a bird with such a piercing look, saucy spiked hair, sky blue feet? The Blue-Footed Booby is a sweetly comical seabird from the Galapagos Islands. When I first saw one, I immediately fell in love. Even more incredible than its looks is the Blue-Footed Booby's talent as a lover. His mysterious allure lies in the movements of his dance. With elegant turns, awkward but rhythmic footwork, and his husky piercing whistle, he wins the heart of his beloved. Spellbound, she will dance the love dance with him. The pair do not gaze longingly into each other's eyes, rather they stare at their heavenly blue feet. Of course, this romantic bird brings tender love tokens as well—small stones, a carefully chosen twig, things that are held dear in booby circles.*

It was immediately obvious that I should write a story about these unusual birds. I sketched out the first ideas while I was still on the tourist boat, going from island to island. I lured my booby away from the Galapagos to the bright lights of the stage, where his dance would seem even more exotic. This was not going to be a book about nature; this was to be an exploration of the nature of love.

Translator's Note: *This bird, called* Tölpel *in German, has a delightful name in English. Their closely set eyes make the birds look cross-eyed when seen head on, and their feet truly are as blue as the sky. Because they look so funny and because of their unusual mating dance, the Spanish called them* bobos *(clowns). The English turned the name into booby.*

Bruno Hächler

Blue-Footed Booby Dance

Illustrated by Cinzia Ratto
Translated by J. Alison James

A Michael Neugebauer Book
North-South Books / New York / London

The director of the concert hall was a very busy man. He did not like interruptions. When someone knocked at his door one morning, he growled, "Enter."

The door opened and in stepped a remarkable bird, with piercing eyes, silly spiked hair, a long brown beak, and the most amazing heavenly blue feet.

The director asked, "What do you want?"

"To dance," replied the bird.

The director wrinkled his forehead. "Dance?"

"Yes," said the bird, "dance." He put his suitcase down, cocked his head to one side, and . . .

He kicked to the left and he kicked to the right.
He hopped in a circle like he might take flight.
He waggle waggle taggled his powerful tail,
And he spun like the wind with his wings as the sail.
Then he stood stock still, his wings cocked wide,
His chest arched up with a show of pride.
He pointed his beak straight up to the ceiling,
And gave a husky whistle—full of feeling.

When he was finished, he picked up his suitcase and waited.

The director had seen many things in his life. But he had never seen a bird who could dance like this. "What is your name?" he asked.

"Booby," said the bird. "Bobby Booby."

"Mr. Booby," the director said, "you've got yourself a job!"

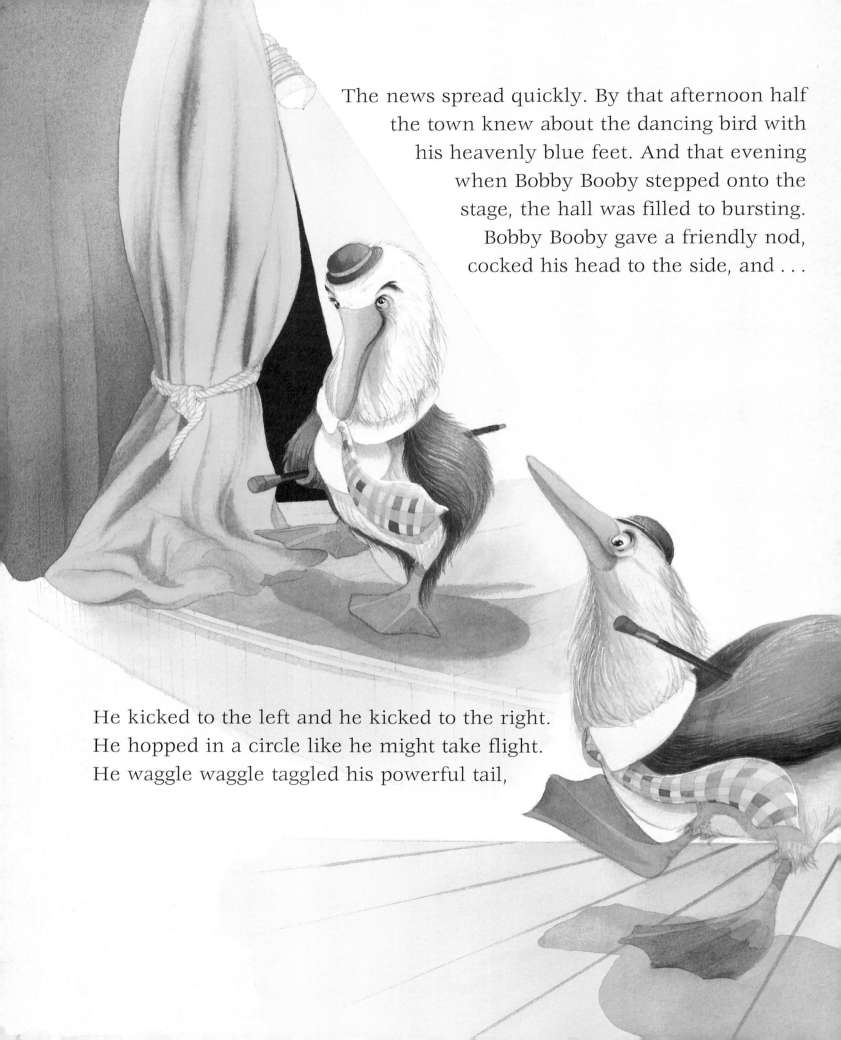

The news spread quickly. By that afternoon half the town knew about the dancing bird with his heavenly blue feet. And that evening when Bobby Booby stepped onto the stage, the hall was filled to bursting. Bobby Booby gave a friendly nod, cocked his head to the side, and . . .

He kicked to the left and he kicked to the right.
He hopped in a circle like he might take flight.
He waggle waggle taggled his powerful tail,

And he spun like the wind
with his wings as the sail.
Then he stood stock still,
his wings cocked wide,
His chest arched up
with a show of pride.
He pointed his beak
straight up to the ceiling,
And gave a husky whistle—
full of feeling.

Thunderous applause roared!

Bobby Booby was *the* sensation. Immediately following the show a newspaper reporter collared him for an interview. Men from the radio were hot on her heels, and the television people elbowed their way through the crowd. Everyone wanted to hear about the famous bird with his heavenly blue dancing feet. The director rubbed his hands with delight.

Bobby Booby was happy too. He loved it when people greeted him on the street. He loved it when children stood in front of the box office, waiting for him to sign autographs. He always brought a stack of photos and he beamed with pride while he signed them with a fat black pen.

It got better and better. There was such a demand for tickets that Bobby Booby had to perform two and three times a day. He started wearing sunglasses on stage so he looked like a star. The director gave him two backup dancers, who twirled around elegantly when he did his whistling act.

That's the way it went—for a while.

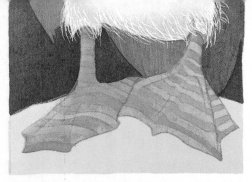

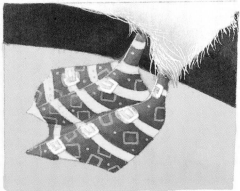

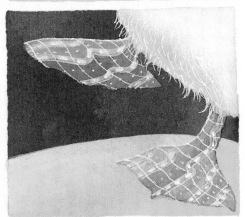

After some time, though, the novelty wore off. Bobby Booby could tell that something had changed. People still came to see him, of course, they still clapped and hooted for him when he danced. But there was a different feeling to their clapping.

One evening, just as he was going to start his dance, someone shouted, "Look, the booby has bluuue feet!"

The audience laughed. Yes, they laughed at him because he was a dancing bird with a husky whistle, and to tell the truth, he really *was* a bit funny. But most of all, they laughed at his big, bright blue feet. Booby Booby felt ashamed.

He decided to disguise his feet for the show and started wearing a variety of socks and shoes, black or red, striped or speckled. Nothing helped. No sooner had the audience taken their seats than the cry started, "Blue-footed Booby! Blue-footed Booby!" Then they roared with laughter. It was humiliating. Bobby Booby became so sad that he couldn't dance properly. He stumbled and missed the beat of the music. Once he even plumped down hard on his feathery bottom. He was so mortified, he wanted to sink right through the floor.

Bobby Booby had had enough. He didn't want to be laughed at any more. He announced that it was the final week of the Bobby Booby Show. Sadly, he left the concert hall and wandered through the streets. But something drew him back.

Bobby Booby gazed at the stage where he had so often danced with joy. There was a knock at the stage door, and in came a small brown duck. Shyly she waddled up to Bobby Booby. "Mr. Booby, you are such a wonderful dancer," she said, blushing. "Even more than your dancing, though, I adore your blue feet. My own feet are so boring. Nobody ever notices them. I wish I had feet like yours!"

Bobby Booby sighed deeply. Trying to comfort him, the duck patted him gently. But it didn't change the way he felt. Bobby Booby was done with dancing.

The next morning, the little brown duck went straight to the shoe store and asked for a pair of shoes in heavenly blue.

"Heavenly blue?" asked the saleslady.

"Heavenly blue," insisted the duck.

A few minutes later the duck left the shop wearing her new pair of shoes. The saleslady knew a good thing when she saw it. She pulled off her own old shoes and slipped into a pair of glorious heavenly blue high heels.

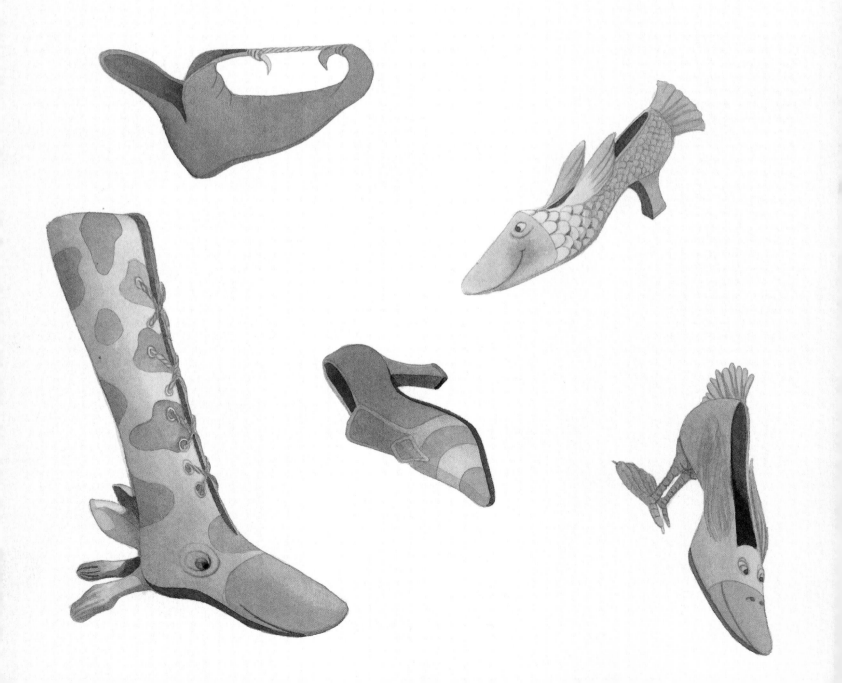

The little brown duck paraded through the city. She went window-shopping, lingering here and there, and at last sat down in a café, with her new blue shoes glinting in the sun. She was showing off. She knew it, and she was pleased. People were noticing her; they were noticing her beautiful shoes. Complete strangers stopped to ask where she'd found such fantastic shoes.

People rushed to the shoe shop and
bought out everything in blue: blue
sandals, blue clogs, blue rubber
boots—they bought anything as long
as it was heavenly blue.
Bobby Booby had no idea about the
little brown duck's blue revolution.
Sick at heart, he moped and waited
for his last performance.

The day came. A sign hung on the door of the concert hall saying:
"Today, Final Appearance of Bobby the Dancing Booby!"

Nervously, Bobby Booby took the stage. He looked around and thought he must be dreaming. People were cheering, so many people that the hall was full to bursting. And every one of them was wearing heavenly blue shoes, the very same hue as his own blue feet.

Bobby Booby hesitated a moment. Then he smiled, kicked off his shoes, pulled off his socks, and tossed them dramatically into the audience. The crowd roared with delight. Bobby Booby cocked his head to one side and started to dance.

He kicked to the left and he kicked to the right.
He hopped in a circle like he might take flight.
He waggle waggle taggled his powerful tail,
And he spun like the wind with his wings as the sail.
Then he stood stock still, his wings cocked wide,
His chest arched up with a show of pride.
He pointed his beak straight up to the ceiling
And gave a husky whistle—full of feeling.

When the applause broke over him, tears of joy streamed down his cheeks. He blew a kiss to the little brown duck who was sitting in the front row.

Then Bobby Booby took bow after bow as flowers were tossed on stage and the audience stomped and cheered. Quietly, the director slipped out and removed the sign from the door.

Bobby Booby was back!